A Note to Parents and Caregivers:

Read-it! Readers are for children who are just starting on the amazing road to reading. These beautiful books support both the acquisition of reading skills and the love of books.

The RED LEVEL presents familiar topics using common words and repeating sentence patterns.

The BLUE LEVEL presents new ideas using a larger vocabulary and varied sentence structure.

The YELLOW LEVEL presents more challenging ideas, a broad vocabulary, and wide variety in sentence structure.

The GREEN LEVEL presents more complex ideas, an extended vocabulary range, and expanded language structures.

When sharing a book with your child, read in short stretches, pausing often to talk about the pictures. Have your child turn the pages and point to the pictures and familiar words. Be sure to reread favorite stories or parts of stories.

There is no right or wrong way to share books with children. Find time to read with your child, and pass on the legacy of literacy.

Adria F. Klein, Ph.D.
Professor Emeritus
California State University
San Bernardino, California

Managing Editor: Bob Temple
Creative Director: Terri Foley
Editor: Peggy Henrikson
Editorial Adviser: Andrea Cascardi
Copy Editor: Laurie Kahn
Designer: Nathan Gassman
Page production: Picture Window Books
The illustrations in this book were rendered with watercolor.

Picture Window Books
5115 Excelsior Boulevard
Suite 232
Minneapolis, MN 55416
1-877-845-8392
www.picturewindowbooks.com

Printed in the United States of America.

Library of Congress Cataloging-in-Publication Data
Blackaby, Susan.
The little mermaid / by Hans Christian Andersen ; adapted by
Susan Blackaby ; illustrated by Charlene DeLage.
p. cm. — (Read-it! readers fairy tales)
Summary: A little sea princess, longing to be human, trades her
mermaid's tail for legs, hoping to win the love of a prince and
earn an immortal soul for herself.
ISBN 1-4048-0221-5
[1. Fairy tales. 2. Mermaids—Fiction.] I. DeLage, Charlene, 1944– ill.
II. Andersen, H. C. (Hans Christian), 1805–1875. Lille havfrue. English.
III. Title. IV. Series.
PZ8.B5595 Li 2004
[E]—dc21
                                                    2003006297

The Little Mermaid

by Hans Christian Andersen

Adapted by Susan Blackaby
Illustrated by Charlene DeLage

Special thanks to our advisers for their expertise:
Adria F. Klein, Ph.D.
Professor Emeritus, California State University
San Bernardino, California

Kathy Baxter, M.A.
Former Coordinator of Children's Services
Anoka County (Minnesota) Library

Susan Kesselring, M.A.
Literacy Educator
Rosemount-Apple Valley-Eagan (Minnesota) School District

PICTURE WINDOW BOOKS
Minneapolis, Minnesota

In the bluest part of the sea stood the Sea King's castle. He lived with his mother and six mermaid daughters. They were beautiful from head to tail.

The sisters played in the gardens. They swam with fish. They loved hearing stories of towns and trees. "Tell us about the rest of the world," they said.

"When you turn 15, you can see it for yourselves," said Grandma. Year by year, each sister swam up to see the land of humans.

At last, the youngest turned 15.
She swam up beside a big ship
floating on the blue-green sea.
On board, sailors sang and danced.

Fireworks lit up the sky. In the glow, the little mermaid saw the face of a handsome prince. She couldn't take her eyes off him.

Suddenly, clouds filled the sky.
Lightning flashed and waves crashed.
The ship broke apart and sank into
the sea. The prince was drowning!

The little mermaid dived under the waves to save the prince. She carried him into a quiet cove. She kissed him and left him on the beach.

The little mermaid hid. Soon a girl came along. The prince woke up and smiled at her. He thought the girl had saved him! This made the mermaid very sad.

The little mermaid returned home but often swam back to look for the prince. She asked Grandma to tell her more about humans.

"They live short, sweet lives on their stumpy little legs," said Grandma. "When they die, their souls rise to the stars and live forever. That's much too long for me."

"How can I get a soul like that?"
asked the little mermaid.

"A human's true love," said Grandma.

"But forget it. Men don't love fish tails."

The little mermaid had to win
the prince's heart. She thought
of the Sea Witch's powers. Bravely,
she swam to the witch's house
made of dead sailors' bones.

"Little fool," said the witch. "You want to trade your tail for a chance at true love? Well, this drink will give you legs. But if you can't win the prince's heart, you'll turn into sea foam."

"I'll do anything!" said the little mermaid. "All right," answered the witch. "But you must give me your sweet voice for the favor. That's fair, don't you think?"

"How can I win the prince's heart
if I can't speak?" asked the little
mermaid. "Charm, charm, charm,"
said the Sea Witch. And with that,
the little mermaid lost her voice.

Before dawn, the little mermaid swam to the cove. She drank the potion and fainted. She woke up to find the prince standing over her.

"Who are you?" asked the prince. The little mermaid couldn't answer. She looked down and saw that her silver tail was gone! She had legs!

The prince took her to the castle.
He gave her fine robes to wear.
From then on, she never left
the prince's side.

The little mermaid loved the prince.
He was fond of her, too. "You remind
me of the girl who saved me,"
he said. "She's my true love."

"I'm the one who saved you!"
the little mermaid wanted to say.
But she had hope. The prince
would never see that girl again.
He'd forget her.

One day the king said to the prince,
"I found you a bride."
"I want only my true love," said
the prince. But then he met the girl
the king had found. She was the girl
on the beach!

"It's *you!*" the prince said to the girl.

"You saved me from drowning!

You are my true love!"

The little mermaid's heart broke in two.

The wedding party was
held on the prince's ship.
The little mermaid knew
she soon would die.
But she smiled, and she
danced more gracefully
than ever before.

Just before dawn, the little mermaid leaned over the ship's rail. Her sisters were there. "We can save you!" they called.

"We traded our hair for the
witch's knife. Use it to kill the prince.
Let his blood drip on your feet.
Your tail will grow back.
You'll come home!"

But the little mermaid could not kill
the prince she loved. She knew
that now she would turn into
sea foam. When the sun rose,
she threw herself into the sea.

To her surprise, the little mermaid felt her spirit rise. She met the daughters of the air. "Spread joy and peace," they said. "You still can earn a human soul and live forever." And so she did.

Levels for *Read-it!* Readers

Blue Level

Little Red Riding Hood, by Maggie Moore 1-4048-0064-6
The Goose that Laid the Golden Egg, by Mark White 1-4048-0219-3
The Three Little Pigs, by Maggie Moore 1-4048-0071-9

Yellow Level

Cinderella, by Barrie Wade 1-4048-0052-2
Goldilocks and the Three Bears, by Barrie Wade 1-4048-0057-3
Jack and the Beanstalk, by Maggie Moore 1-4048-0059-X
The Ant and the Grasshopper, by Mark White 1-4048-0217-7
The Fox and the Grapes, by Mark White 1-4048-0218-5
The Three Billy Goats Gruff, by Barrie Wade 1-4048-0070-0
The Tortoise and the Hare, by Mark White 1-4048-0215-0
The Wolf in Sheep's Clothing, by Mark White 1-4048-0220-7

Green Level

The Emperor's New Clothes, adapted by Susan Blackaby 1-4048-0224- X
The Lion and the Mouse, by Mark White 1-4048-0216-9
The Little Mermaid, adapted by Susan Blackaby 1-4048-0221-5
The Princess and the Pea, adapted by Susan Blackaby 1-4048-0223-1
The Steadfast Tin Soldier, adapted by Susan Blackaby 1-4048-0226-6
The Ugly Duckling, adapted by Susan Blackaby 1-4048-0222-3
Thumbelina, adapted by Susan Blackaby 1-4048-0225-8